To Grandma for always saying yes to one more game.
And to my kids, may you always find the joy in life!
xoxoxo

Books & Things Publishing, LLC

Virginia

978-1-7357218-3-5

To help support the author, don't forget to leave a review, and share your love of this book with your friends and family via social media and tag @daniellemariettabooks.
Visit daniellemariettabooks.com and subscribe to the seasonal newsletter. Scan the code below for more information and other books by Danielle Marietta.

Manufactured in the United States
Booksandthingspublishing.com
Cover and interior design by Sarah Jane Docker

MR. MALOOF

Written by Danielle Marietta
Illustrated by Sarah Jane Docker

Mr. Maloof was a silly guy,
his mother used to say.
He'd hide and play tricks
from sun up to sun down
each and every day.

He'd **pop** out from behind the curtains
or even the bathroom door.
One day he hid under the rug
in the middle of the living room floor.

"Little Maloof, you're such a goof!

One day you will see.
Not everything is a trick,
but rather real as real can be!"

"Silly mommy, what do you know?
I'll be doing tricks as long as I grow!"

"Ok Mr. Maloof, but what happens when you're old?
One day you will stop growing and these tricks will be too **bold**."
Never will that happen, he thought.

Until that thought festered
and grew quite a lot.

And then one day it happened.
He was goofy no more.

He didn't plan schemes
that involved popping out
from the floor.

The day had actually come,
as his mother said it would.
There were no jokes to tell,
not even if he could.

A frown on his face stretched
from his left ear to his right.
It was the **frowniest frown**
that anyone had seen that night.

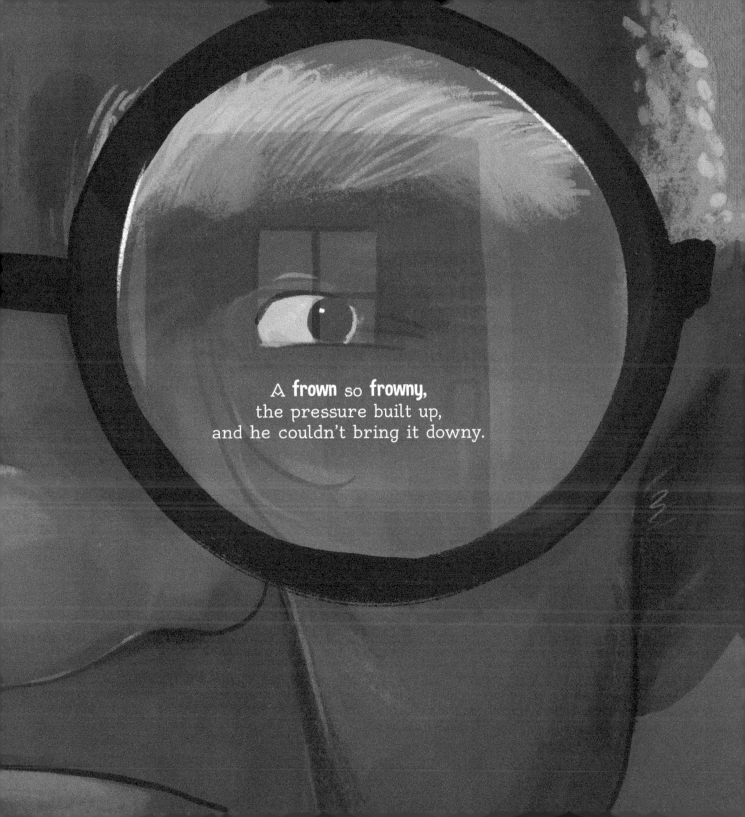

A **frown** so **frowny,**
the pressure built up,
and he couldn't bring it downy.

And out it sprouted, one single hair,
not enough for the smallest of pony.

But, oh, what was this?
This color up here.
There was no doubt, it was crystal clear.
A sliver of color just above his right ear.

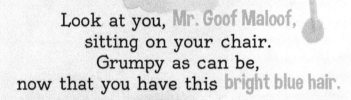

Look at you, Mr. Goof Maloof,
sitting on your chair.
Grumpy as can be,
now that you have this bright blue hair.

You *huff* **and** pout

and stomp about

wondering how this came to be.
It wasn't there a week ago.
Not one, two or even three.

Not brushing nor combing, crimping nor curling would tame this little blue beast.

There it stood, up on his head, pointing 87 degrees northeast.

There he was thinking thoughts
on how to make this quite **quick**.
He could **pluck** it with tweezers, or
snip it with clippers.

Yes, that would do the trick!

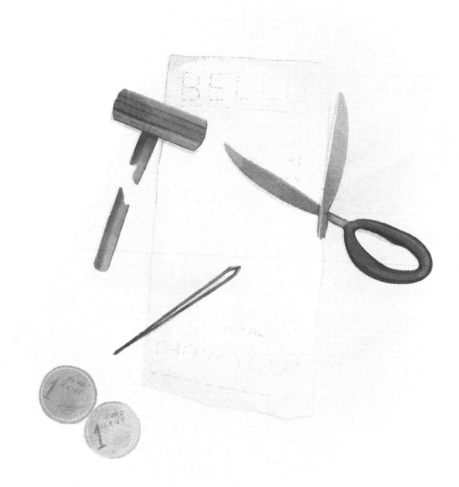

But when he tried to **trim** and **cut**,
his clippers all broke and he had zero luck.

Then he jumped up and out.
"A hat!" he said, "will permanently cover this
obnoxious little blue on my head!"

That afternoon the old **Mr. Maloof**
sat rocking on his stoop.
Until three young kids came
passing by and said, **"Hey there you old goof!"**

They laughed and teased until the old man sneezed and his blue hair **burst** right on through.

The hat stood no chance when it came down to it.
"What bad luck,
I should have knew it!"

Then one kid yelled,
"His hair is blue!"
"No way, that can't be true."

The oldest kid pulled off her hat and
blue hair fell right down her back.

Mr. Maloof sat still in shock.
They waved and continued on around the block.
They'll be back, he knew and planned out just what he'd do.

A prank of all pranks.
They won't know what hit 'em.
I'll hide in the bushes then shout,

"Blue bliggum!"

Days came and went but there he stayed, determined not to move.
Then one day, here they came strolling straight down his avenue.

When the moment was right,
he struck, oh he struked!
And those kids yelled out with all their might.

A moment of silence, and everyone laughed.
"What's your name old man?" they asked curiously.

"Mr. Maloof is what my mother has always called me."

"We'll get you next time you silly old *goof!*"

And they did.
   And they did.

And they did.
   And they did.

Although Mr. Maloof had grown quite old,
his silliness was an art.
And that little blue hair that showed up that day,
reminded him we are always young at heart.

CPSIA information can be obtained
at www.ICGtesting.com
Printed in the USA
BVHW021541100322
631153BV00012B/270